Little Lions

JIM ARNOSKY

G.P. PUTNAM'S SONS ❖ NEW YORK

G. P. Putnam's Sons, Reg. U.S. Pat. & Tm. Off. Published simultaneously in Canada.
Printed in Hong Kong by South China Printing Co. (1988) Ltd.
Text set in Zapf International
Library of Congress Cataloging-in-Publication Data
Arnosky, Jim. Little lions/Jim Arnosky. p. cm.
Summary: On a rocky ledge, two baby mountain lions play and purr
and meow under the protection of their mother.
1. Pumas—Juvenile fiction. [1. Pumas—Fiction.2. Animals—Infancy—Fiction.]
I. Title. PZ10.3.A68923Li 1998 [E]—dc21 96-49837 CIP AC
ISBN 0-399-22944-2 10 9 8 7 6 5 4 3 2 1 First Impression

For Denise

On a brilliant April afternoon,
high up on a rocky ledge,

a mountain lion lies
resting in the sun.

She is not alone.
She has two babies,
just four weeks old.

Their mother gives them
everything they need.

She keeps them warm.
She feeds them milk.

She protects them
from strangers.

She lets them play on her.

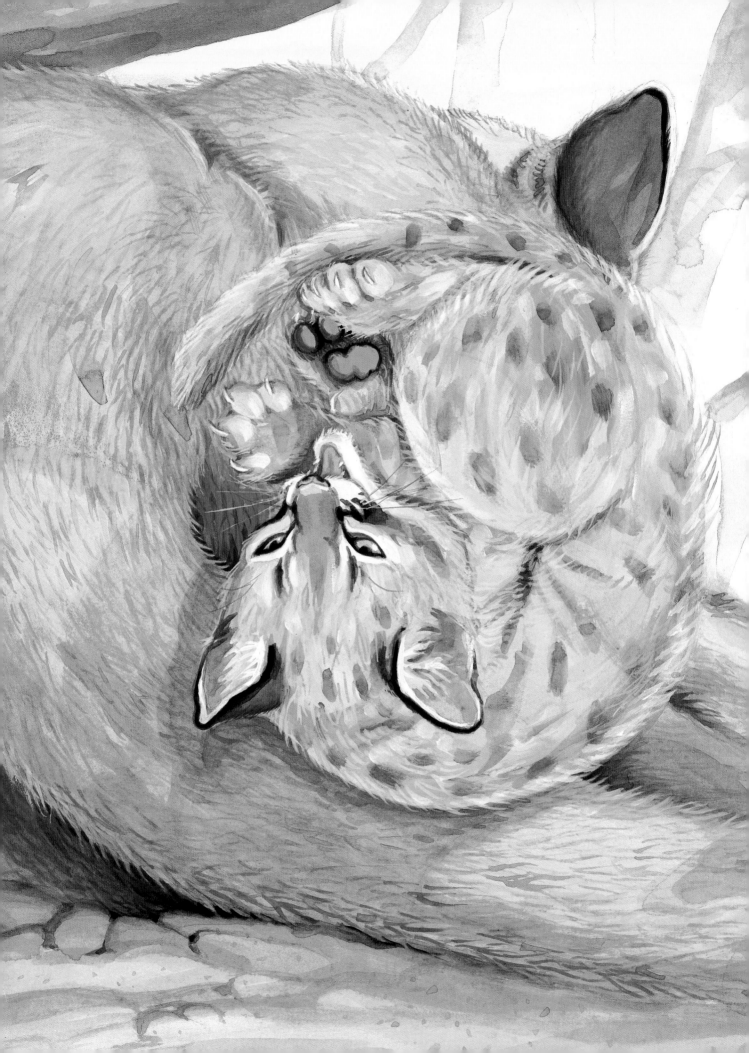

The little lions climb
mother's hilly hips,
and tumble down her tail.

They jump over
giant lion legs.

They wrestle near
great big lion jaws.

Little lions dig down
under mother's chest . . .

. . . and crawl out
between her paws.

They creep and peek

over the ledge edge.

Soon they'll leave
the ledge to wander
with their mother.

She'll teach them
how to hunt.

But now they're only
kittens, on a sunny
mountain step . . .

. . . playing, purring,
and meowing, with
mother always near.